*All children have
a great ambition to read
to themselves...*

*and a sense of achievement when they can do so.
The* **read it yourself** *series has been devised to
satisfy their ambition. Since many children learn
from the Ladybird Key Words Reading Scheme,
these stories have been based to a large extent
on the Key Words List, and the tales chosen are
those with which children are likely to be familiar.*

*The series can of course be used as supplementary
reading for any reading scheme.*

The Enormous Turnip *is intended for children
reading up to Book 2c of the Ladybird Reading
Scheme. The following words are additional to the
vocabulary used at that level —*

old, man, turnip, seeds, plants,
grow, one, enormous, dinner, pull,
up, but, can't, calls, woman, help,
me, boy, us, she, girl, cat, mouse,
all, carry

*A list of other titles at the same level will be
found on the back cover.*

Published by Ladybird Books Ltd Loughborough Leicestershire UK
Ladybird Books Inc Lewiston Maine 04240 USA

The Enormous Turnip

adapted by Fran Hunia
from the traditional tale
illustrated by John Dyke

Ladybird Books

This old man has some turnip seeds.

Turnip

5

The old man plants the seeds.

7

He waters the seeds.

The turnip seeds
grow.

One turnip grows
and
grows
and
grows!

It is
enormous!

The old man says,
I want some turnip
for dinner.

He goes to pull up
the enormous turnip.

He pulls and pulls,
but he can't pull up
the enormous turnip.

The old man calls
to the old woman.
Come and help me
to pull up
this enormous turnip,
he says.

The old woman pulls
the old man
and the old man pulls
the turnip.
They pull and pull,
but they can't pull up
the enormous turnip.

The old woman calls
to a boy.
Come and help us
to pull up
this enormous turnip,
she says.

The boy pulls
the old woman
and the old woman
pulls the old man
and the old man
pulls the turnip.
They pull and pull,
but they can't pull up
the enormous turnip.

The boy calls
to a girl.
Come and help us
to pull up
this enormous turnip,
he says.

The girl pulls the boy
and the boy pulls
the old woman
and the old woman
pulls the old man
and the old man
pulls the turnip.

They pull and pull,
but they can't pull up
the enormous turnip.

The girl calls
to a dog.
Come and help us
to pull up
this enormous turnip,
she says.

The dog pulls
the girl
and the girl pulls
the boy
and the boy pulls
the old woman
and the old woman
pulls the old man
and the old man
pulls the turnip.

They pull and pull,
but they can't pull up
the enormous turnip.

The dog calls
to a cat.
Come and help us
to pull up
this enormous turnip,
he says.

The cat pulls
the dog
and the dog
pulls the girl
and the girl
pulls the boy
and the boy pulls
the old woman

and the old woman
pulls the old man
and the old man
pulls the turnip.
They pull and pull,
but they can't pull up
the enormous turnip.

The cat calls
to a mouse.
Come and help us
to pull up
this enormous turnip,
she says.

The mouse pulls
the cat
and the cat pulls
the dog
and the dog pulls
the girl
and the girl pulls
the boy

and the boy pulls
the old woman
and the old woman
pulls the old man
and the old man
pulls the turnip.
They pull and pull
and . . .

up comes
the enormous turnip!

They all help
to carry the turnip
home.

And they all have turnip for dinner.